SCIENCE COURT

TO SERVE AND OBSERVE™

The Case of the Late Great Kaboom!

Adapted by Craig Strasshofer

Based on an original TV episode written and created by Tom Snyder, Bill Braudis, and David Dockterman

Illustrated by Bob Thibeault and Kristine Koob

Troll

THE SOUND OF SILENCE

On a starry summer night, the residents of Sciville were gathered on the town common. They had come for the big bicentennial celebration, which was to begin at exactly midnight. It seemed like everyone in town was there. There were balloons, amusement rides, carnival booths, and people—people laughing, playing, eating hot dogs and cotton candy. A stage had been set up in front of the courthouse, and on that stage were most of the town's important citizens. A huge banner was draped across the front of the stage that read: "Sciville Bicentennial

Party—200 Years in the Making."

It was almost midnight, and the feeling of excitement grew as people pressed close to the large stage, waiting for the opening ceremony to begin. Off to one side of the crowd, Sasha Meany talked feverishly into her cellular phone. Sasha was the event coordinator. She was good at her job. She was also a pushy person. Maybe that's why she was such a good event coordinator—she knew how to get things done.

"Look, it's almost midnight," she said urgently into the phone. "That cake had better be delivered here. I want this to be the best bicentennial celebration this town's ever had. What? Oh, I know it can have only one bicentennial. That's not the point. The point is, you'd just better not be late."

As she snapped the phone shut, one of her assistants scurried forward with a plastic cup full of steaming coffee. "Here's your

coffee, Ms. Meany," he said.

"Where on earth have you been?" Sasha demanded. "I asked for this black coffee two minutes and twenty-seven seconds ago."

"Sorry," the assistant apologized.

"How's Shep doing with the cannon?" Sasha asked.

"He was fine the last time I talked to him," said the assistant.

Sasha glanced at her watch. "It's three minutes until midnight. I want that cannon to be fired just at the stroke of midnight, not one second before or after. The entire celebration depends on the cannon being fired at exactly the right time."

"I understand," the assistant replied.

"The cannon will be shot," Sasha went on, "then the balloons will be released, the fireworks will go off, the band will start playing . . ." She paused to sip her coffee, then made a sour face. ". . . and I will have a fresh cup of coffee in my hand. But everything starts with the cannon."

Meanwhile, on a hilltop just outside of town, Shep Sherman stood next to an old cannon. He was enjoying the warm summer night, as he viewed the town below and watched an occasional shooting star fly across the sky. *I wonder if I have time for a quick thirty-second nap*, he thought to himself. Then he closed his eyes and relaxed.

A few moments later, Shep opened his eyes and looked at his watch. "Nah." He shook his head. "I wouldn't feel refreshed."

Back at the party, J. C. Cramwood had stepped up to the microphone on the stage. Cramwood was Sciville's biggest and only resident movie star, which made him very happy. "As the town's biggest and only movie star, it's my job to start the countdown," he announced. "Is everybody ready?"

"Yeah!" the crowd shouted out.

"Shep had better be ready," Sasha muttered to herself.

"Okay," said Cramwood.

Sasha, staring at the second hand on her watch, whispered, "Go."

Together, Cramwood and the crowd began the countdown. "Ten, nine, eight . . ."

Sasha's assistant rushed up to her. "Shep's on the phone!" he exclaimed.

"Just tell him to get ready to fire the cannon," Sasha yelled.

The countdown continued, ". . . three, two, one . . ."

And then came . . . nothing! Just the silence of a summer night, broken only by the squawking of several birds, which sounded strangely like laughter.

"Shep's late," Sasha groaned. "I can't believe it."

J. C. Cramwood put his acting skills to work, crying out with nervous enthusiasm, "Okay, let's try it again! Three, two, one . . ."

Again there was nothing but silence.

J. C. Cramwood was crushed. "Oh, no," he said, "the party's ruined."

But just at that moment came the roar of the cannon booming out across the valley. The crowd let out a huge cheer. The balloons were released, the fireworks went off, and the band began to play.

Cramwood turned to Sasha. "Boy, that was close. I thought we were starting the big two-hundredth anniversary without the cannon. But it worked out okay."

Suddenly a peculiar-looking character in an orange jumpsuit seemed to fall from the sky, landing right on the stage. His parachute came floating down behind him, covering the heads of Cramwood and several other important people. The strange sky diver took off his helmet to reveal a mop of wild hair.

"Great entrance," Cramwood said to the stranger.

"Thank you," answered the stranger. "Great party."

"It's not great," Sasha fumed. "It's not perfect. I told Shep to fire the cannon at exactly the stroke of midnight."

The sky diver was impressed. "Wow. He was pretty close."

"Pretty close doesn't cut it with me," Sasha said. "I have personally organized some of the biggest celebrations in the country—presidential inaugurations, big high-society weddings, and kids' parties."

"Really?" said the man. "Kids' parties?"

"This tarnishes my reputation," Sasha pouted. "It could ruin me."

"Well," the man observed, "maybe with a little solvent and some sandpaper I can shine that reputation back up for you. Or if that doesn't work, we can get you a new one."

AN INAUGURATION IS A FORMAL CEREMONY THAT'S HELD WHEN SOMEONE ASSUMES AN ELECTED POLITICAL OFFICE.

I KNEW THAT.

Sasha didn't understand. "What?" she asked.

The strange character thrust out his hand and smiled broadly. "Allow me to introduce myself. I'm Doug Savage, Science Court attorney. I think I may be able to help."

Just then a gust of wind caught Doug's parachute, and he was whisked back up into the air. Cramwood and Sasha watched as he floated off into the distance, like a kite when the string breaks.

SOME SOUND ADVICE

A few days later, Shep Sherman was sitting in the office of Science Court's finest defense attorney, Alison Krempel, along with her trusty assistant, Tim.

"I can't believe I'm being sued," Shep said. "This is crazy, isn't it?"

"I'm afraid not," Alison replied, leafing through some official-looking documents to make sure she hadn't overlooked anything. "Apparently Sasha Meany blames you for firing the cannon late, ruining her carefully planned celebration and putting a blemish on her spotless reputation."

"But I had a great time at the party," Shep said, "and I think that's what everyone is going to remember."

"Well, Sasha wants you to admit publicly that it was your fault the cannon was fired late," Alison explained. "She wants you to take out a full-page ad in the newspaper."

"Wow, me in the newspaper," said Shep. At first he thought that would be wonderful, since he'd never been in the newspaper before. Then the hard facts hit. "But wait a minute! That would cost a lot of money. And I didn't do anything wrong. I fired the cannon at exactly twelve midnight."

"Exactly?" Tim asked.

"Exactly?" Alison repeated.

"Exactly," Shep insisted.

"Shep," said Alison, "do you realize that you were thirty-seven minutes late for our meeting today?"

"Oh. Well . . . yeah," said Shep. "Sorry

about that. I'll hang around for thirty-seven minutes after you leave tonight to make up for it."

"That won't be necessary," Alison said.

"No. I insist," Shep argued.

"Shep, it's all right," said Alison. "Let me ask you something. You weren't late with the cannon because you wanted to get back at Sasha, were you?"

"No!" Shep denied.

"We know she can be pretty difficult," Alison said understandingly.

"Sure she's pretty," Shep exclaimed, "and difficult. But I fired the cannon on time, Ms. Krempel. I don't know why everyone didn't hear it until ten seconds later."

"I do," Tim said.

"You do?" Shep asked.

"Sure." Tim nodded. "It all has to do with the way sound travels."

"Oh," said Shep. "So, will you help me?"

"Yes, Shep," Alison replied. "We'll help you. In fact, because Tim knows so much about it, I'm going to let him do a lot of the questioning."

"Oh, thank you, Ms. Krempel. Thank you. I'll do great, really. I won't let you down," Tim promised.

"I know you won't, Tim," Alison said with a smile. "I know you won't."

3

THE LATE SHEP SHERMAN

On the day of the trial, Micaela hurried to make it to the courthouse on time. Micaela was a young girl who loved Science Court. She'd never missed a Science Court trial, and she was eager to see this one. As she approached the courthouse, she noticed Stenographer Fred, the official Science Court stenographer, sitting on the front steps. He was eating doughnuts and drinking coffee, and he didn't look well.

"Hi, Fred," Micaela said.

"Hi, Micaela," Fred replied.

"How are you?" Micaela asked.

"Not too good," answered Fred. "My wrist is a little sore."

"Sorry to hear that," Micaela said.

"But not as bad as my shoulder," Fred added.

"Oh," said Micaela.

Fred went on with his tale of woe. "And my thumb hurts when I bend it all the way back. Like this." He bent his thumb back until it hurt, then cried out in pain, "Stop that, Fred!"

"Uh hmm," Micaela mumbled.

"And my hair sort of hurts a tiny bit . . . and then I fell . . ." Fred went on and on.

"Okay, whatever," said Micaela. "I'll see you inside."

Micaela went in, and Fred followed behind, still complaining about his many aches and pains. The courtroom was packed. Doug and his client, Sasha, sat together across the aisle from Alison and Tim. Their client, Shep, was nowhere in sight. Micaela squeezed into the front row of the gallery for a good view, while Fred hurried to the stenographer's desk. He took his seat just before Science Court reporter Jen Betters began her broadcast.

"Hello and welcome to Science Court, where science is the law and scientific thinking rules. I'm Jen Betters reporting, and today we have a case that I hear will be very interesting. Oh, look, here comes Judge Stone now."

"All rise," said Fred, feeling a bit dizzy. "But not too fast. You'll get dizzy." Then he fell over.

Judge Stone entered the courtroom and took her seat at the bench. "Okay. Thank you, Stenographer Fred," she began as he sat up. "Welcome, everyone. So, why don't we get right to it? Mr. Savage, you're representing Sasha Meany, is that correct?"

"Yes, that's right, Your Honor," Doug replied.

"And, Ms. Krempel," Judge Stone went on, "you're representing Shep Sherman. Is he here?"

"No, Your Honor. He's late," answered Alison.

"Guilty. The trial's over," Doug shouted. Then he turned to Sasha and whispered, "Start walking toward the door."

All eyes in the crowded courtroom were on Doug and Sasha as they tried to get up and walk out without being noticed.

"Mr. Savage," Judge Stone called firmly, "just because the man is late doesn't mean he's guilty. Get back to your seats. We still have to have a trial."

"Oh, all right," Doug said as he and Sasha reluctantly returned to their places.

"And let's start with your opening statement," the judge went on.

"Okay," Doug said, as he approached the jury box. "Ladies and gentlemen of the jury, we will show that Shep Sherman, the man who is late today—late to his own trial—was also late in firing the cannon on the night of the bicentennial and ruined the celebration."

"Oooooh . . ." said one juror.

"Ahhhh . . ." said another.

"I had a fantastic time," remarked Judge Stone.

"Objection," Doug objected. "I believe that statement is biased against my client and ask that the jury disregard it."

"Mr. Savage, you're absolutely right," Judge Stone admitted. "When you're right, you're right. I ask the jury to disregard my comment."

The members of the jury mumbled quietly among themselves.

"What comment?" one asked.

"I didn't hear anything," another said.

23

"What did you say?" asked a third.

Judge Stone leaned over and whispered to Stenographer Fred, "You've got to love this jury." Then she raised her voice and said, "Continue, Mr. Savage."

"Thank you," said Doug. "Because Shep was late, Sasha Meany's reputation has been sullied, soiled, stained, tarnished, dirtied, blemished, and . . . wait just a minute . . . sullied, soiled, stained, tarnished, dirtied, blemished . . . I guess that's it."

"Thank you, Mr. Savage," said Judge Stone.

"Ruined!" Doug shouted out. "That's it! Sullied, soiled, stained, tarnished, dirtied, blemished, and ruined."

"Okay, I think we've got it," said Judge Stone. "Thank you. Now, Ms. Krempel, your opening statement, please."

"Thank you, Your Honor." Alison rose from her seat and began. "We will show that

25

my client, Shep Sherman, fired the cannon at exactly the right time and that there is a logical scientific explanation for the ten-second delay."

"Sounds good," Judge Stone said. "Mr. Savage, call your first witness."

"Thank you, Your Honor," Doug replied. "I call Sasha Meany to the stand."

Sasha took the witness stand, and Doug began his line of questioning.

"Ms. Meany," Doug said, "at what time was the cannon supposed to be fired on the night in question?"

"At twelve midnight. Exactly," Sasha answered.

"And what time did you actually hear the boom from the cannon?" asked Doug.

"Ten seconds after midnight," Sasha told him.

A murmur rose from the jury box.

"Thank you," Doug said. "That's all."

"Wait a minute," Sasha called. "Aren't you going to ask me how this botched event will affect my business?"

"You already told me," said Doug.

"Shouldn't I tell the jury, too?" Sasha suggested.

"Oh, they don't want to hear about all that," Doug replied with a shrug. Then he turned to the jurors and asked, "Do you?"

"Sure," they said. "Why not? We're already here."

"Okay." Doug shrugged once again as he turned back to Sasha. "Go ahead."

"Well," said Sasha, "my reputation is at stake. Because of Shep's error, I could lose millions of dollars in future jobs."

"There, did you hear that?" Doug asked the jury. "Thank you."

Suddenly Alison's assistant, Tim, spoke up. "Your Honor, may I please question the witness?"

28

"Yes, Tim, go right ahead," Judge Stone replied.

"Ms. Meany, what makes you so sure that Shep didn't fire the cannon at exactly midnight?" Tim asked Sasha.

"We didn't hear the boom until ten seconds after midnight," Sasha replied.

"And all of the clocks and watches were synchronized?" Tim asked.

"Yes," Sasha answered firmly.

"Does that mean you put them in the sink?" Doug interrupted.

Everyone began to snicker at what they thought was a funny play on words. They didn't know Doug was being serious.

"No," Tim said. "'Synchronized' means that all of the clocks showed exactly the same time."

"Oh, yeah, right . . . synchronized," Doug mumbled. "I thought you said . . . uh . . . shminktinized."

"We know, Mr. Savage, we know," said Judge Stone. "Is that all, Tim?"

"Yes, Your Honor," Tim responded.

"Okay, then," the judge declared. "The witness may step down. Mr. Savage, call your next witness."

"For my next witness," Doug said with a smirk, "I call . . . Shep Sherman! I said, Shep Sherman . . . yoo-hoo, Shep Sherman. Has anyone seen Shep Sherman? Oh, where could he be? I'll tell you where he is. He's guilty. That's where he is!"

Just then Shep came dashing into the courtroom. "Hey, everybody. Sorry I'm late," he said, huffing and puffing.

MAKING WAVES

Shep's late arrival to the courtroom had Alison worried. "Shep, what happened?" she whispered. "This doesn't look good."

"You mean the shirt?" Shep asked.

"No . . . oh, never mind," Alison said, shaking her head. "Please take the stand."

As soon as Shep was settled, Doug Savage began his questioning. "Shep, please tell this courtroom what time it was when you fired the cannon the night of the bicentennial celebration."

"It was midnight," said Shep. "Exactly."

"Twelve midnight?" Doug asked.

"That's the only midnight I know of," said Shep.

"Oh, right," Doug answered sheepishly. "Well, how come the boom of the cannon wasn't heard until a full ten seconds after midnight?"

"I guess it has to do with the way sound travels," Shep replied.

"Objection," Doug objected.

"Doug, are you objecting to the witness answering your own question?" Judge Stone asked.

"Oh . . ." said Doug, "that doesn't make sense, does it? Why don't we just forget I said that? Stenographer Fred, please strike that from the record."

"I don't have to," said Fred. "I didn't write it."

Doug decided to try a different angle with the witness. "Shep, isn't it true that you wrote a letter to the newspaper that said

something about time and relaxing?"

"Well, yeah," Shep admitted. "I just want people to stop rushing around and to start living 'in the moment.' You know, to really appreciate what they have now."

"So in other words, you think people are controlled by the clock, is that right?" Doug probed.

"Yes," said Shep.

"Is that why you were late in firing the cannon?" asked Doug.

"I wasn't late," Shep insisted. "I told you, it has something to do with the way sound travels."

"But I was there," said Doug. "I heard the shot at ten seconds after midnight, with my own ears. Your Honor, this is about as open and shut as a case can get."

"I assume then that you're resting your case?" Judge Stone said.

Doug chuckled. "Oh, I'm doing more

than just resting my case, Your Honor. I'm tucking it in and kissing it good night."

"Wonderful," said Judge Stone. "Okay, Ms. Krempel, you're up."

"Thank you, Your Honor," Alison said, approaching the witness stand. "Shep, please tell us what happened on the night in question."

"Well," Shep replied, "I was up on the hill with the cannon. I was keeping a close eye on my watch, even though I don't like doing that. At exactly midnight I hit the button and the cannon went off."

"Did it make a sound?" Alison asked.

"Oh, yeah," said Shep, "a loud boom. It sounded like a cannon going off."

J. C. Cramwood, who was watching the trial from the gallery, leaped to his feet and cried, "BOOM! That's the way I heard it."

"Thank you," said Alison to both of them. "Your Honor, I now call sound-wave expert Professor Parsons to the witness stand."

Professor Parsons was Science Court's resident expert on everything. He took the stand and sat there waving to the crowd. "Top o' the mornin', all. Hello. How are you? I'm waving because I'm a waving wave expert. Get it? Waving wave expert."

"Thank you, Professor Parsons," Alison said. She gave him a few moments to stop laughing at his own joke, then went on, "Could you please explain how sound gets from one place to another?"

"Ahh . . . what?" asked the professor.

"I said, can you show us how sound—"

"I'm sorry, what?"

Alison began to get annoyed and raised her voice. "I said, can you please show us how sound waves—"

"Yes, yes, I heard you." Professor Parsons laughed at himself again. "I'm kidding. It's a sound joke. See, you said 'sound,' and I said 'what,' as if I didn't hear you."

"I get it," Alison sighed.

"Come on, group, lighten up," said the professor. "Life's too short."

"That's what I told them," Shep chimed in.

"Let's keep this moving," Judge Stone ordered. "Could you answer the question?"

"Oh, certainly, certainly," replied the professor. "That's what I'm here for, right? Answering the questions. Luckily I brought my handy tank of water with me today." He pointed to the big tank of water perched on a table next to the witness stand and pulled a pencil out of his pocket. "All right. Let's say this pencil that I'm poking the water with is the cannon. You see the little waves moving away from the pencil?"

"Yes," answered Doug.

"I was talking to the jury," said Professor Parsons.

"Oh," said Doug.

"Well, anyway," the professor went on, "if this pencil was indeed a cannon going off, those water waves would be similar to sound waves leaving the cannon."

"You really lost me this time," Doug grumbled. "Stenographer Fred, could you read that back to me, please?"

"Um, okay," said Fred. "Let's see . . . 'cannon the leaving waves sound to similar be would waves water those'. . ."

"No, Fred," Judge Stone broke in. "He didn't mean read it backward."

"Oh, sorry," Fred apologized. "Let me try again. 'If this pencil was indeed a cannon going off, those water waves would be similar to sound waves leaving the cannon.'"

"Objection," Doug shouted.

"What? I read it right," Fred defended himself.

"Maybe pencils can make water waves,

but sound is invisible and fast and can't make waves like that," said Doug.

"Yes, it can," said Alison.

"No, it can't," Doug argued.

"Yes, it can," repeated Alison.

"No, it can't," Doug persisted.

"Yes, it can," Alison repeated again.

"Yes, it can," said Doug.

"I know it can," confirmed Alison.

"You're supposed to say it can't," Doug challenged.

Judge Stone banged her gavel. "Order, order!" she bellowed. "Okay, you two, stop making waves. The question is: Can sound make waves in the air like Professor Parsons' pencil made waves in the water?"

"I'm already finished thinking about it," said Doug.

"Well, think about it some more," Judge Stone commanded. "Science Court is now in recess."

The judge banged her gavel again, and Jen Betters instantly put the microphone to her mouth and turned toward the camera. "Boy," she said quickly, "we've heard a lot of questions about sound. We'll hear some of the answers in a moment."

Just then, J. C. Cramwood came into view on TV screens all over Sciville. "Ask me a question about my new movie," he said, smiling into the camera.

"I'm sorry, but do I know you?" Jen replied.

GOOD VIBRATIONS

Soon the courtroom was filled with people again. They were mumbling among themselves as they waited patiently for the trial to resume. Judge Stone took her seat and banged her gavel to restore order.

"Court's in session, no more noise," said Stenographer Fred. "Not even this, like what I'm doing now."

"Thank you, Stenographer Fred," said Judge Stone. "Now, the question is: Can sound make waves like waves in water? Professor Parsons, can you help us out here?"

"Absolutely," said Professor Parsons as he

pulled a tuning fork out of his pocket. "I am holding a tuning fork. Tapping this will produce a small musical tone."

He tapped the tuning fork on the table, producing a small musical tone. The jurors were amazed.

"Ooh!" they exclaimed in unison.

"And why do we hear that sound?" Tim asked.

"The tuning fork vibrates and creates sound waves that travel to our ears," said Professor Parsons.

"And what does this have to do with water?" Tim asked.

"I tap it, put it in the water, then . . ." Professor Parsons demonstrated as he spoke. ". . . the vibrations make waves. Not sound waves, but water waves that act much like sound waves. Oh, it all works out."

"Thank you, Professor," said Tim. "No more questions."

"But I have some questions," said Doug.

"Well, then, you can cross-examine," Judge Stone replied.

"What does that mean again?" Doug asked.

"You can ask more questions," Judge Stone explained.

"Oh, that's right. I love that." Doug smiled and turned to the professor. "So, Professor Parsons, we meet again."

"I don't like your tone, young man," Professor Parsons said. "No, I guess we do meet again. I'm kidding."

"Professor, if that really is your name, you are saying that sound is a wave like water waves are waves. Correct?" Doug asked.

"Correct," said the professor.

"And water waves go through water. Correct?" Doug asked.

"Right again," the professor replied.

"So if sound is a wave, it has to travel

46

through some stuff that can get all wavy," said Doug.

"Ah, yes, that's right," Professor Parsons agreed.

"What if I told you that's nothing but a pack of lies?" asked Doug.

This question caught Professor Parsons off guard. "Huh?" he said.

Doug pulled a huge gong and a mallet out from under his jacket and said, "I have a big gong here. Micaela, would you be so kind as to bang the gong for me, please?"

"Sure," said Micaela. "Everybody get ready."

Micaela hit the gong, and its sound rang out loud and long. Doug started talking, but no one could hear him. They could only see his mouth moving and his arms waving around. Finally, the sound faded away. Everyone was covering both ears.

"Ouch," cried a juror.

"Thank you," Doug concluded.

"Mr. Savage, would you repeat what you were just trying to say?" said Judge Stone. "And next time you plan to make a loud noise, please warn us."

"Oh, sorry," Doug replied. "Well, what I said was, there's no 'stuff' between the jury and the gong, but they still heard the sound. How did the wavy sound waves wave over there?"

"Mr. Savage, you're missing the point here," said Professor Parsons.

"You're wrong, Professor, when you say that sound travels in waves and has to go through something," Doug stated.

"Me, wrong? What? Why, that's just ridiculous," Professor Parsons spluttered.

"Well," said Doug, "there's nothing here for the waves to go through. No water, no nothing. Only air."

"Exactly," said Professor Parsons.

"Exactly what do you mean by 'exactly'?" Doug asked smugly.

"Mr. Savage, what are you breathing?" the professor responded even more smugly.

"Uhh . . . air?" Doug guessed.

"Right," said Professor Parsons. "Air is the stuff that sound waves move through."

"I love air!" J. C. Cramwood cried out.

"Oh, now I've heard everything," Doug scoffed. "I didn't see any wavy waves rolling around the courtroom. Did you, jury?"

"No," said one jury member.

Another replied, "All I heard was the gong."

"I'm still hearing the gong," said yet another.

Satisfied with the jury's response, Doug went on. "I've seen waves crashing on the beach. I've seen waves in my bathtub. I've even seen amber waves of grain. But I've never seen waves in the air."

"Professor," Alison asked, "do you have another example that might help?"

"Oh, sure, I have plenty of examples," the professor said. "Plenty of examples. I'm full of them."

Professor Parsons put an old-fashioned alarm clock in a vacuum jar and pumped out the air.

"What are you doing?" Doug asked.

"I'm removing the air from this jar with the alarm clock inside of it," the professor explained. "Now, the alarm is set to go off in about . . . three, two . . . now!"

The alarm clock began shaking and vibrating inside the jar, but no sound came out.

"Boy, that's what I need," Shep Sherman commented, "a silent alarm clock."

"But I don't hear anything," said Doug. "What's going on?"

"Well, I'm going to explain it to you,"

the professor assured him. "Sound waves need to move through something, like air, to get to our ears. You can actually feel the sound waves going through the air if you stand next to a car with the radio cranked up. Oh, yeah, play that funky music."

"Okay, okay. I get it now," Doug said. "I call Micaela to the stand."

A VACUUM JAR IS ALSO CALLED A BELL JAR. IT'S A GLASS CONTAINER WITH A ROUNDED TOP AND AN OPEN BASE. YOU CAN PUMP ALL THE AIR OUT AND PERFORM SCIENTIFIC EXPERIMENTS.

"What?" Micaela exclaimed in surprise. She loved watching Science Court trials, but she'd never been a witness before.

"It will only take a minute," Doug told her.

Micaela took the witness stand.

"Micaela," Doug said.

"What?" Micaela asked again.

"Thank you, that's all," said Doug. "See, Micaela heard me call her name at the exact moment I said it because sound moves through the air so fast, you can't even measure it."

"Yes, you can," Alison objected. "Your Honor, Mr. Savage doesn't know what he's talking about."

"So?" replied Doug.

"He's right, Ms. Krempel," said Judge Stone. "It doesn't matter. It's his case. Continue, Mr. Savage."

"Thank you," Doug said confidently.

"Shep's cannon was late because it was fired late. And I'm about to prove it."

In his hands he held two clocks. One was an alarm clock. The other was not. "I will give this clock to Micaela and ask her to hold it. Then I will ask Fred to put the alarm clock way up in the rafters at the back of the courtroom."

"Are you crazy?" said Fred. "I'm not going up there."

"Are you afraid of heights?" Doug asked.

"No. I'm afraid of falling," Fred said.

"Then get me a ladder and I'll put it up there myself," Doug persisted.

"Doug, make sure that the two clocks are synchronized," Tim cautioned.

Doug held the clocks up so everyone could see that they both read exactly 11:55. "They're synchronized," he said. "The alarm clock is set to go off in five minutes." Shakily, he climbed to the top of the ladder

54

and placed the alarm clock on a rafter near the ceiling. *Boy, this is really high,* he said to himself. But he made it back down safely and returned to the front of the courtroom. Everyone waited in silence as they watched the clock Micaela was holding. The big hand ticked over to the next minute, and at exactly the same time the alarm went off at the back of the room.

The jury was impressed.

"Oooh!"

"Wow, that was fast!"

"How's he going to get it down?"

"Yes! Yes!" Doug cried out with glee. "See, the sound waves from the alarm clock moved so fast they were instantaneous. At the same moment this clock struck twelve, we heard the alarm from the other one. Sound moves fast, not slow like waves. Now I really rest my case. Ms. Krempel, I suggest you do the same."

"Hardly," Alison said. "Your Honor, with the court's permission, I'd like to do a short demonstration of my own."

Judge Stone turned to the jurors. "What do you think?" she asked.

"Yeah, sure." They all nodded. "The more the merrier. Demonstrate away."

"All right, then," Judge Stone agreed. "Carry on, Ms. Krempel."

"Thank you," said Alison.

Tim handed Alison a gong and two clocks.

"Now, Stenographer Fred, will you give us a hand, please?" Alison asked.

"As long as I don't have to climb up a ladder," said Fred.

"You don't," Alison assured him. "Just a hill. Carry this gong and this clock outside, up to the top of Courthouse Hill."

"But that's a mile away," said Fred.

"That's right," Alison told him. "I want

you to bang the gong at exactly one o'clock."

"You mean like this?" Fred asked. And with that he banged the gong. All the spectators shook in their seats and covered their ears.

"Whew," said Alison. "At least we know how loud the gong is, right, Mr. Savage?"

Doug still had his fingers in his ears. "What?" he mumbled.

"Micaela, would you like to go with Stenographer Fred and help him?" Alison asked.

"Yes, ma'am," said Micaela.

"Now, Tim, synchronize the clocks," Alison instructed.

Tim adjusted the clocks and then held them up so everyone could see that they read exactly the same time.

"Give one to Micaela and Stenographer Fred, and they can start walking," Alison went on.

"I have to warn you," Fred said to Micaela, "I get car sick."

"We're not driving," Micaela explained. "We're walking."

"Well," said Judge Stone, "why don't we take a short recess while Micaela and Fred climb Courthouse Hill." Again she banged her gavel. "Science Court is adjourned."

Through the window, Fred and Micaela could be seen heading up Courthouse Hill. Fred was struggling under the weight of the heavy gong. Micaela took the gong and gave the clock to Fred. Micaela carried the gong with ease.

Jen Betters turned to the camera and held up her microphone. "And there they go," she said. "But to do what? We'll be back in a few minutes to find out."

THE GONG SHOW

Before long Science Court was back in session. As Judge Stone took her place at the bench, some people noticed that she seemed to be crying a bit. She blew her nose loudly and said, "I'm sorry, it's just that I miss Fred already." She blew her nose again and wiped one last tear from her eye. "Okay, sorry. I'll be all right. What now, Ms. Krempel?"

Alison was holding a stopwatch. "I'm going to time it," she said.

"Time what?" Doug asked.

"You'll see," Alison replied. "Okay, it's almost time."

Meanwhile, Fred and Micaela were waiting at the top of the hill. Fred was out of breath from the climb, but Micaela seemed in good condition.

"Boy, that was tough," Fred wheezed.

"Are you all right?" Micaela asked.

"I'm a little woozy," said Fred, "but I'll be fine."

Micaela watched the clock as Fred stood by, ready to bang the gong.

"It's almost time," Micaela said. "Ready, Freddy?"

"Yep," said Fred.

Micaela began the countdown. "Three . . . two . . . one . . . hit it!"

Fred hit the gong at exactly one o'clock. Back in the courtroom, nothing was heard except the quiet click of Alison starting the stopwatch.

"Hey," Doug exclaimed, "they didn't hit it on—"

Just at that moment, a faint gonging sound was heard, and Alison stopped the timer.

"—time," Doug finished.

"Five seconds," said Alison, looking at the stopwatch.

"What?" asked Doug.

"Tim, do you have your calculator with you?" Alison asked.

"Sure," Tim told her, as he pulled a calculator out of his pocket.

"Okay," said Alison. "If Fred is one mile away and the sound took five seconds to get here, how long would it take sound waves to travel through the air between the cannon and the town common, which are two miles apart?"

"That's easy," said Doug. "Uh . . ."

"Ten seconds," said Tim.

The jury's reaction was intense.

"Wow."

"Ten seconds."

"That's how late Shep was."

"I'm hungry."

"Tim, about how fast would those sound waves be traveling?" Doug asked.

Tim worked it out on his calculator. "Around seven hundred miles an hour," he said. "Or about three hundred meters per second."

Again the jury reacted intensely.

"Wow."

"That's fast."

"I can't even run that fast."

"I love the metric system."

"Seven hundred miles an hour? But that's illegal, isn't it?" Doug inquired.

"Not for sound, Doug," Tim replied.

"Well, very impressive demonstrations," said Judge Stone. "How about topping it off with some closing comments? Mr. Savage, give it your best shot."

"Thank you, Your Honor," Doug said.

In the best lawyer voice he could muster, he began what sounded as if it was going to be a very long speech. "Two hundred years ago, this town was just a couple of log cabins, a few dead horses, and a dream . . ."

"The short version, please," said Judge Stone.

"Shep's guilty," said Doug.

"Thank you, Mr. Savage." Judge Stone turned to Alison. "Ms. Krempel, your closing argument, please."

"Thank you," Alison answered. "Shep Sherman believes that sometimes we need to slow down and enjoy life—not be such slaves to the clock. And I agree. But regardless of how Shep feels about clocks and time, the fact is he did fire the cannon at exactly twelve midnight on the night of the celebration. But because he was two miles away from the town common, nobody heard the cannon until ten seconds after midnight.

Sound travels in waves, at more than seven hundred miles an hour through air. That's roughly five seconds a mile."

Doug started to put earplugs in his ears.

"Why are you putting those in?" Sasha whispered. "Are there going to be more loud noises?"

"You'll see," Doug replied mysteriously.

"When sound goes from point 'A' to point 'B,'" Alison continued, "it's not instantaneous. The sound moves like water waves moving through the ocean. The waves take their own time with their own wavy motion."

"Okay," Judge Stone said. "Well, jurors, the case is all yours. Go and deliberate until your hearts are content." She banged her gavel. "Science Court is adjourned until the jury reaches a verdict."

A SOUND VERDICT

Everyone filed out of the room and stood around in the hallway. Once again, Jen Betters faced the camera. "Well, the jury has the case," she said. "Let's talk to some of the participants while we wait. Here's Shep Sherman. Shep, how do you think the case will go?"

"Well," said Shep, "I think the scientific laws of sound will prove I'm right."

"Wow! It sounds like you've learned something," Jen commented. "Oh, and here's Sasha Meany."

Sasha came over to Jen. Next to Sasha

was Doug Savage, with enormous earplugs sticking out of his ears.

"Ms. Meany, what do you think of your case?" Jen inquired.

Sasha just pointed to Doug and asked, "Is this guy for real?"

"Afraid so," Jen said. Suddenly she held her hand up to the tiny receiver in her ear. "Oh, I just got word the jury has reached a verdict."

Everyone dashed back to the courtroom to hear the outcome of the case. Judge Stone was already at the bench. "Okay, jury," she said, "let me hear you."

Doug Savage was sitting with his fingers, legs, and arms crossed.

"Are you superstitious?" Sasha asked.

"No," Doug answered. "I'm just really unlucky."

The jury foreperson stood up and announced the verdict. "Judge Stone, we, the jury, find the defendant not guilty."

"Yeah!" Doug almost shouted.

"But I'm not the defendant," Sasha reminded him.

"Oh. Well, want to pretend you are?" Doug asked.

"Why for cryin' out loud!" exclaimed Sasha.

"Thank you, jury," said Judge Stone. "Great job."

"And one more thing," the foreperson continued.

"Of course."

"The evidence shows that Shep fired the cannon on time, but because of the way sound travels, it only appeared that he fired it late," the foreperson said.

"Well, thanks for clarifying that," Judge Stone said.

"One more thing?"

"Sure," replied the judge, putting on her

motorcycle jacket and sunglasses as she got ready to leave the bench. "I live alone. Nobody's expecting me."

"We feel that Sasha could have figured out in advance that the cannon should be fired ten seconds early," the foreperson said.

"A good point," Judge Stone agreed. "Done?"

"Done," said the foreperson.

"Fred, dismiss Science Court," ordered the judge. "Fred? Fred? Oh, that's right. Fred's not here. Well, then, I'll do it myself. Science Court is adjourned." And with that she banged her gavel to close the case of the late great kaboom.

A GOOD SOUND SLEEP

Later that evening, after everyone else had gone home, Fred and Micaela were still sitting on top of Courthouse Hill, waiting for someone to tell them to come down. They had made a little campfire and were toasting marshmallows. Fred was telling a story, and Micaela was bored.

"Yeah," said Fred, "most kids just dream about becoming a stenographer. But I did something about it."

"Uh-huh," Micaela mumbled, yawning.

"Because I'm a doer. I take the bull by the horns," Fred added, enjoying his subject.

"A stenographer has to be a doer."

"Right," said Micaela.

"But the key is not to do too much," Fred continued.

"Didn't you say earlier that you were feeling woozy?" Micaela asked. "I am," she sighed as she drifted off to dreamland.

"Yeah, I guess," Fred recalled. "But I'm feeling a lot better now. In fact, I . . . I . . ." He yawned as the campfire died. Then his eyelids slowly fluttered shut, and he began to snore.

Things That Go Boing!

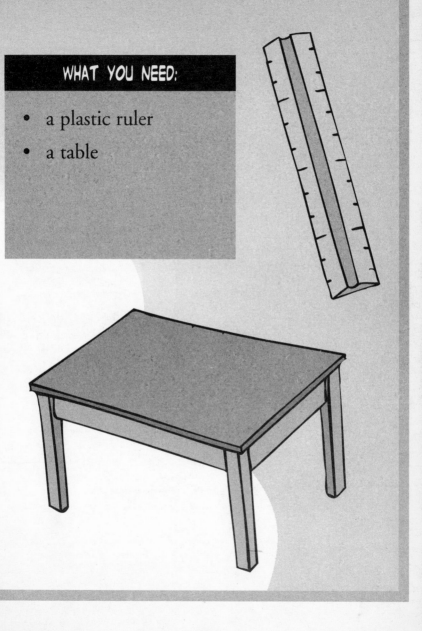

WHAT YOU NEED:

- a plastic ruler
- a table

1

Put the ruler flat on a tabletop with as much of the ruler hanging over the edge of the table as possible.

2

Using the palm of your hand, tightly hold down the part of the ruler that's on the table.

WHAT HAPPENS:

As the part of the ruler hanging over the table edge gets shorter, the pitch of the sound gets higher.

3

Use your other hand to push the free end of the ruler down. Then, with one quick motion, let it go back up.

4

With the free end of the ruler vibrating up and down, move the palm of your hand quickly so that more of the ruler slides onto the table.

5

Listen to the way the sound changes.

WHAT IT PROVES:

Sound is made when something vibrates. The faster the object vibrates, the higher the pitch of the sound will be. The slower the object vibrates, the lower the pitch of the sound will be.

For more Science Court fun, and to find out how to bring Science Court into your classroom, visit our web site.
www.TeachTSP.com/classroom/SciCourt